PIG GETS LOST

There is a little yellow duck to find on every page.

This is Apple Tree Farm.

This is Mrs Boot, the farmer. She has two children called Poppy and Sam, and a dog called Rusty.

Mrs Boot has six pigs.

There is a mother pig and five baby pigs. The smallest pig is called Curly. They live in a pen.

Mrs Boot feeds the pigs every morning.

She takes them two big buckets of food.
But where is Curly? He is not in the pen.

She calls Poppy and Sam.

"Curly has got out," she says. "Please come and help me to find him."

"Where are you, Curly?"

Poppy and Sam call to Curly. "Let's look in the hen run," says Mrs Boot. But Curly is not there.

"There he is, in the barn."

"He's in the barn," says Sam. "I can just see his tail." They all run into the barn to catch Curly.

"That's not Curly."

"It's only a piece of rope," says Mrs Boot. "Not Curly's tail." "Where can he be?" says Poppy.

"Let's look in the cow shed."

But Curly is not in the cow shed. "Don't worry," says Mrs Boot. "We'll soon find him."

"Perhaps he's in the garden."

They look all round the garden but Curly is not there. "I think he's lost for ever," says Sam.

"Why is Rusty barking?"

Rusty is standing by a ditch. He barks and barks.
"He's trying to tell us something," says Poppy.

"Rusty has found Curly."

They all look in the ditch. Curly has slipped down into the mud and can't climb out again.

"We'll have to lift him out."

"I'll get into the ditch," says Mrs Boot. "I'm coming too," says Poppy. "And me," says Sam.

Curly is very muddy.

Mrs Boot picks Curly up but he struggles. Then he slips back into the mud with a splash.

Now everyone is very muddy.

Sam tries to catch Curly but he falls into the mud.
Mrs Boot grabs Curly and climbs out of the ditch.

They all climb out of the ditch.

"We all need a good wash," says Mrs Boot.
"Rusty found Curly. Clever dog," says Sam.

THE HUNGRY DONKEY

This is Apple Tree Farm.

This is Mrs Boot, the farmer. She has two children called Poppy and Sam, and a dog called Rusty.

There is a donkey on the farm.

The donkey is called Ears. She lives in a field with lots of grass, but she is always hungry.

Ears, the donkey, is going out.

Poppy and Sam catch Ears and take her to the farmyard. Today is the day of the Show.

Ears has a little cart.

They brush her coat, comb her tail and clean her feet. Mrs Boot puts her into her little cart.

Off they go to the Show.

Poppy and Sam climb up into the little cart. They all go down the lane to the show ground.

"You stay here, Ears,"

At the show ground, Mrs Boot ties Ears to a fence. "Stay here. We'll be back soon," she says.

Ears gets free.

Ears is hungry and bored with nothing to do. She pulls and pulls on the rope until she is free.

Ears looks for food.

Ears trots across the field to the show ring. She sees a bunch of flowers and some fruit.

"That looks good to eat."

She takes a big bite, but the flowers do not taste very nice. A lady screams and Ears is frightened.

Ears runs away.

Mrs Boot, Poppy and Sam and the lady run after her and catch her. "Naughty donkey," says Sam.

Ears is in disgrace.

"I'm sorry," Mrs Boot says to the lady. "Would you like to take Ears into the best donkey competition?"

Ears is very good now.

The lady is called Mrs Rose. She climbs into the cart. "Come on," she says and shakes the reins.

Ears trots into the show ring.

She trots round the ring, pulling the cart. She stops and goes when Mrs Rose tells her.

Ears wins a prize.

"Well done," says the judge and gives her a rosette. He gives Mrs Rose a prize too. It is a hat.

It is time to go home.

Mrs Rose waves goodbye. "That was such fun," she says. Ears trots home. She has a new hat too.

TRACTOR
IN TROUBLE

This is Apple Tree Farm.

This is Mrs Boot, the farmer. She has two children, called Poppy and Sam, and a dog called Rusty.

Ted works on the farm.

He helps Mrs Boot. Ted looks after the tractor and all the farm machines.

Today it is very windy.

The wind is blowing the trees about and it is very cold. Poppy and Sam play in the barn.

"Where are you going, Ted?"

Ted is driving the tractor out of the yard. "I'm just going to see if the sheep are all right," he says.

Ted stops the tractor by the gate.

He goes into the sheep field. He nails down the
roof of the sheep shed to make it safe.

Poppy and Sam hear a terrible crash

"What's that?" says Sam. "I don't know. Let's go and look," says Poppy. They run down the field.

"A tree has been blown down."

"It's come down on Ted's tractor," says Poppy.
"Come on. We must help him," says Sam.

"What are you going to do, Ted?"

Poor Ted is very upset. The tree has scratched his new tractor. He can't even get into the cab.

"Ask Farmer Dray to help."

"Go and ask your Mum to phone Farmer Dray,"
says Ted. Poppy and Sam run to the house.

Soon Farmer Dray comes with his horse.

Farmer Dray has a lovely big carthorse, called Dolly. They have come to help Ted.

"I'll cut up the tree first."

Farmer Dray starts up his chain saw. Then he cuts off the branches which have fallen on the tractor.

Dolly starts to work.

Farmer Dray ties two ropes to Dolly's harness.
Ted ties the other ends to the big branches.

Dolly pulls and pulls.

She works hard until all the branches are off the tractor. "Well done, Dolly," says Farmer Dray.

Ted climbs up into the cab.

"Thank you very much, Farmer Dray and Dolly," he says. And they all go back to the farmyard.

The tractor looks a bit of a mess.

Ted finds a brush and paints over all the scratches.
"It will soon be as good as new," he says.

THE GRUMPY GOAT

This is Apple Tree Farm.

This is Mrs Boot, the farmer. She has two children called Poppy and Sam, and a dog called Rusty.

Ted works on the farm.

He tells Poppy and Sam to clean the goat's shed.
"Will she let us?" asks Sam. "She's so grumpy now."

Gertie the goat chases Sam.

She butts him with her head. He nearly falls over.
Sam, Poppy and Rusty run out of the gate.

Poppy shuts the gate.

They must get Gertie out of her pen so they can get to her shed. "I have an idea," says Sam.

Sam gets a bag of bread.

"Come on, Gertie," says Sam. "Nice bread."
Gertie eats it and the bag but stays in her pen.

"Let's try some fresh grass," says Poppy.

Poppy pulls up some grass and drops it by the gate. Gertie eats it but trots back into her pen.

"I have another idea," says Sam.

"Gertie doesn't butt Ted. She wouldn't butt me if I looked like Ted," says Sam. He runs off again.

Sam comes back wearing Ted's clothes.

He has found Ted's old coat and hat. Sam goes into the pen but Gertie still butts him.

"I'll get a rope," says Poppy.

They go into the pen. Poppy tries to throw the rope over Gertie's head. She misses.

Gertie chases them all.

Rusty runs out of the pen and Gertie follows him.
"She's out!" shouts Sam. "Quick, shut the gate."

Sam and Poppy clean out Gertie's shed.

They sweep up the old straw and put it in the wheelbarrow. They spread out fresh straw.

Poppy opens the gate.

"Come on, Gertie. You can go back now," says Sam. Gertie trots back into her pen.

"You are a grumpy old goat," says Poppy.

"We've cleaned out your shed and you're still grumpy," says Sam. "Grumpy Gertie."

Next morning they meet Ted.

"Come and look at Gertie now," says Ted. They all go to the goat pen.

Gertie has a little kid.

"Oh, isn't it sweet," says Poppy. "Gertie doesn't look grumpy now," says Sam.

THE NEW PONY

This is Apple Tree Farm.

This is Mrs Boot, the farmer. She has two children, called Poppy and Sam, and a dog called Rusty.

Mr Boot, Poppy and Sam go for a walk.

They see a new pony. "She belongs to Mr Stone, who's just bought Old Gate Farm," says Dad.

The pony looks sad.

Her coat is rough and dirty. She looks hungry.
It looks as though no one takes care of her.

Poppy tries to stroke the pony.

"She's not very friendly," says Sam. "Mr Stone says she's bad tempered," says Mr Boot.

Poppy feeds the pony.

Every day, Poppy takes her apples and carrots.
But she always stays on the other side of the gate.

One day, Poppy takes Sam with her.

They cannot see the pony anywhere. The field looks empty. "Where is she?" says Sam.

Poppy and Sam open the gate.

Rusty runs into the field. Poppy and Sam are a bit scared. "We must find the pony," says Poppy.

"There she is," says Sam.

The pony has caught her head collar in the fence.
She has been eating the grass on the other side.

Poppy and Sam run home to Mr Boot.

"Please come and help us, Dad," says Poppy. "The pony is caught in the fence. She will hurt herself."

Mr Boot walks up to the pony.

He unhooks the pony's head collar from the fence.
"She's not hurt," says Dad.

"The pony's chasing us."

"Quick, run," says Sam. "It's all right," says Poppy, patting the pony. "She just wants to be friends."

They see an angry man. It is Mr Stone.

"Leave my pony alone," says Mr Stone. "And get out of my field." He waves his stick at Poppy.

The pony is afraid of Mr Stone.

Mr Stone tries to hit the pony with his stick. "I'm going to get rid of that nasty animal," he says.

Poppy grabs his arm.

"You mustn't hit the pony," she cries. "Come on Poppy," says Mr Boot. "Let's go home."

Next day, there's a surprise for Poppy.

The pony is at Apple Tree Farm. "We've bought her for you," says Mrs Boot. "Thank you," says Poppy.

SCARECROW'S SECRET

This is Apple Tree Farm.

This is Mrs Boot, the farmer. She has two children, called Poppy and Sam, and a dog called Rusty.

Mr Boot is working in the barn.

"What are you doing, Dad?" asks Sam. "I'm tying lots of straw on these poles," says Mr Boot.

"What is it?"

"You'll soon see," says Dad. "Go and get my old coat from the shed, please. Bring my old hat too."

"It's going to be a scarecrow."

Poppy and Sam come back with the coat and hat.
Then they help Mr Boot put them on the scarecrow.

"He's just like a nice old man."

"I've got some old gloves for him," says Sam.
"Let's call him Mr Straw," says Poppy.

"He's finished now."

"Help me carry him, please, Poppy," says Mr Boot. "You bring the spade, Sam."

They all go to the corn field.

Mr Boot digs a hole in the field. Then he pushes the pole in so that Mr Straw stands up.

"He does look real."

"I'm sure Mr Straw will scare off all the birds," says Sam. "Especially the crows," says Poppy.

Mr Straw is doing a good job.

Every day Mr Boot, Poppy and Sam look at Mr Straw. There are no birds in the corn field.

"There's Farmer Dray's scarecrow."

"He's no good at all," says Sam. "The birds are eating all the corn and standing on the scarecrow."

"Why is Mr Straw so good?"

"Sometimes he looks as if he is moving," says
Poppy. "His coat goes up and down. It's very odd."

"Let's go and look."

"Let's creep up very quietly," says Sam. And they tiptoe across the corn field to look at Mr Straw.

"There's something inside his coat."

"It's moving about," says Poppy. "And it's making a funny noise. What is it?" says Sam.

"It's our cat and her kittens."

Carefully they open the coat. There is Whiskers, the cat, and two baby kittens hiding in the straw.

"So that's scarecrow's secret."

"Whiskers is helping Mr Straw to frighten off the birds," says Poppy. "Clever Mr Straw," says Sam.

First published in 1993 by Usborne Publishing Ltd. Usborne House, 83-85 Saffron Hill, London EC1N 8RT Copyright © 1993, 1992, 1990 Usborne Publishing Ltd.